Notes for adults

TADPOLES ACTION RHYMES are structured to provide support for newly independent readers. The books may also be used by adults for sharing with young children.

The language of action rhymes is often already familiar to an emergent reader, so the opportunity to see these rhymes in print gives a highly supportive early reading experience. The alternative rhymes extend this reading experience further, and encourage children to play with language and try out their own rhymes.

If you are reading this book with a child, here are a few suggestions:

1. Make reading fun! Choose a time to read when you and the child are relaxed and have time to share the story.
2. Recite the rhyme together before you start reading. What might the alternative rhyme be about? Why might the child like it?
3. Encourage the child to reread the rhyme, and to retell it in their own words, using the illustrations to remind them what has happened.
4. Point out together the rhyming words when the whole rhymes are repeated on pages 12 and 22 (developing phonological awareness will help with decoding) and encourage the child to make up their own alternative rhymes.
5. Give praise! Remember that small mistakes need not always be corrected.

First published in 2010 by
Franklin Watts
338 Euston Road
London NW1 3BH

Franklin Watts Australia
Level 17/207 Kent Street
Sydney NSW 2000

Text (Five Little Penguins)
© Brian Moses 2010
Illustration © Mark Chambers 2010

The rights of Brian Moses to be identified as the author of Five Little Penguins and Mark Chambers as the illustrator of this Work have been asserted in accordance with the Copyright, Designs and Patents Act, 1988.

ISBN 978 0 7496 9371 8 (hbk)
ISBN 978 0 7496 9377 0 (pbk)

Series Editor: Melanie Palmer
Series Advisors: Dr Hilary Minns and Catherine Glavina
Series Designer: Peter Scoulding

Printed in China

Franklin Watts is a division of Hachette Children's Books an Hachette UK company. www.hachettelivre.co.uk

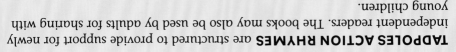

Five Little Monkeys

Retold by Brian Moses

Illustrated by Mark Chambers

W

FRANKLIN WATTS

LONDON•SYDNEY

Mark Chambers

"Keep monkeying around and, like the penguins, eat up your fish!"

Five little monkeys
jumping on the bed.

One fell off and
bumped his head.

Mama called the doctor
and the doctor said,

"No more monkeys
jumping on the bed!

10

No more monkeys
jumping on the bed!"

Five Little Monkeys

Five little monkeys

jumping on the bed.

One fell off and

bumped his head.

Mama called the doctor

and the doctor said,

"No more monkeys jumping on the bed!

No more monkeys jumping on the bed!"

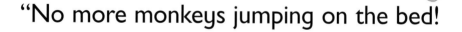

Can you point to the
rhyming words?

Five Little Penguins

by Brian Moses
Illustrated by Mark Chambers

Brian Moses

"I've never been very good at sliding in the snow. I was always the child who fell over!"

Five little penguins learning how to slide.

One slips up and
hurts his side.

17

Mama called his Papa

and his Papa cried,

19

"No more penguins learning how to slide!

No more penguins
learning how to slide!"

Five Little Penguins

Five little penguins

learning how to slide.

One slips up and hurts his side.

Mama called his Papa

and his Papa cried,

"No more penguins learning how to slide!

No more penguins learning how to slide!"

Can you point to the rhyming words?

Puzzle Time!

How many fish can you
see in this picture?

Answers

There are seven fish
in this picture.